IN OUR GARDEN

by **PAT ZIETLOW MILLER**

illustrated by **MELISSA CROWTON**

G. P. Putnam's Sons

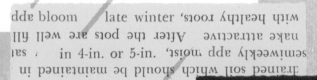

For Ron Harrell and Gladys Veidemanis—teachers
who helped me see what could be. —P.Z.M.

For those who nurture, be it plant or person.
And for my mom and dad, who do both. —M.C.

G. P. Putnam's Sons
An imprint of Penguin Random House LLC, New York

First published in the United States of America by G. P. Putnam's Sons, an imprint of Penguin Random House LLC, 2022
Text copyright © 2022 by Pat Zietlow Miller | Illustrations copyright © 2022 by Melissa Crowton

Library of Congress Cataloging-in-Publication Data | Names: Miller, Pat Zietlow, author. | Crowton, Melissa, illustrator.
Title: In our garden / by Pat Zietlow Miller; illustrated by Melissa Crowton. | Description: New York: G. P. Putnam's Sons, 2022.
Summary: Students create a vegetable garden on their school's rooftop. | Identifiers: LCCN 2021000930 (print) |
LCCN 2021000931 (ebook) | ISBN 9781984812100 (hardcover) | ISBN 9781984812117 (epub) | ISBN 9781984812124 (kindle edition)
Subjects: CYAC: Gardens—Fiction. | Gardening—Fiction. | Schools—Fiction. | Classification: LCC PZ7.M63224 In 2022 (print) |
LCC PZ7.M63224 (ebook) | DDC [E]—dc23 | LC record available at https://lccn.loc.gov/2021000930 | LC ebook record available at
https://lccn.loc.gov/2021000931

MANUFACTURED IN THE USA | ISBN 9781984812100 | 10 9 8 7 6 5 4 3 2 1 | PC

Design by Eileen Savage | Text set in Yoga Sans Pro | The art was done in a mixture of traditional and digital mediums.

It's a day. A gray day.
A breakfast-can-wait, don't-be-late day.
I look out my window and see concrete.
Steps and stoops. Sidewalks and streets.
Everything is hard. And dull.
Not like where I used to live.
Most days, I feel gray too. Homesick, my mom says.

But today, I have an idea.
Something to make this gray place more like home.
Just thinking about it makes me bounce.
My idea is soft. And bright.
My idea is green and orange and red and white.
My idea is a garden.

"A garden?" asks Kianna. "At school?"

"Why?" asks Nico.

"To grow things," I say. "Like carrots. Or cauliflower."

"Oh," says Nico. "I like flowers."

He looks down.

"No," I say. "Look up."

He does. At rooftops and clouds.

Kianna shrugs. "There's no space, Millie.
Gardens can't hang from the sky."
I feel gray again.
Until I remember.
They see what is. I see what could be.
I see a garden.

We're in class. Science class.
What-a-plant-needs-besides-seeds class.
But we don't have plants. Just worksheet words.
I raise my hand. And wave it.
"We need a garden," I say.

I tell everyone how I used to live in a tall building—
more than an ocean away.
I helped my family grow food. On our roof.
Cabbages. Radishes. Carrots.
And cauliflower. Which isn't a flower at all.

There's no garden at our new apartment.
We don't have the right kind of roof.
So we eat store-bought carrots that don't taste like home.

I tell them this school has a fine flat roof.

A roof made for a garden.

No one says anything.

Not even Miss Mirales.

Maybe I shouldn't have shared.

Maybe, in America, gardens only grow on the ground.

Then Miss Mirales says:
"To have a garden, we'd need supplies."
Suddenly, everyone has ideas.

Just like that, I'm bouncing again.

ROOF ←

But it takes more than ideas
to build a garden.

Gardens take work. Hard work.

Lift-high-and-lug, pull-and-tug work.

Parents and neighbors bring piles of supplies.

"This will be a garden?" asks Nico.
He can't see it. But I can.

Kianna measures.

Miss Mirales saws.

Then we all build.

While we work, Principal Blinson talks.
She says gardens bring people together.

Soon, it's time to plant.
Kianna wants cabbages.
Nico wants cauliflower.
He thinks it will look like a daisy.
I choose carrots, of course.
Soil spills. And water.
We all make mud.
Everyone laughs. Even Miss Mirales.
I'm not sure if this is togetherness.
But it's a start.

After weeks of watching, our garden is empty.
"Come on, carrots!" I whisper.
"Be patient," says Miss Mirales.
"Good things take time."

Every day, I wish for something green.
But there's only brown.

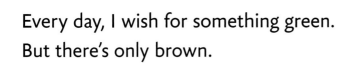
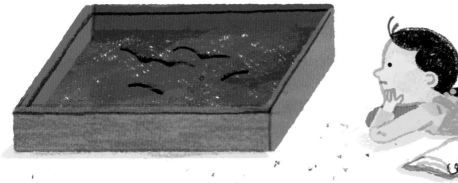

Still, there's plenty to do.
We measure sunlight and rain.
Track the temperature.
We spell C-A-B-B-A-G-E.
C-A-U-L-I-F-L-O-W-E-R.
C-A-R-R-O-T.
And read about gardens.

Miss Mirales talks about roots. Sprouts.
And *germination*.
She says the seeds in our garden are changing.
Maybe I'm changing too.
Maybe I'm like our seeds.
Stuck in new soil. Hoping to grow.

I've almost given up, when I see something.
A weed?
NO!

A sprout?
YES!
Nico laughs.
Kianna cheers.

I bounce around and find more sprouts.
Miss Mirales smiles like she's always known
that this was a garden waiting to grow.

Check out this garden. Our garden!
Our high-in-the-sky, thought-we'd-try garden.
Nico pushes a wheelbarrow. Kianna pulls weeds.
I water everything. And whisper, "Grow, plants, grow!"

Now everyone wants to see our glorious garden.

And take some of it home!

We fill bags. With green and orange and red and white.

Because once plants start growing, they keep right on going.

Miss Mirales and Principal Blinson hand out vegetables.

And tell everyone the garden was my idea.

I look down.
Same sidewalk. Same street.
I look up.
Same clouds. Same sky.
But everything's different.
Everything's better.

Kianna grabs a cabbage
and sniffs Nico's cauliflower bouquet.
I find the sunniest carrot and take a bite.
It tastes like home.
Right here, in our garden.